For Nicole & Alicia   B.M.

For Cathy   S.L.

A NICE SURPRISE FOR FATHER RABBIT

by BRIAN MANGAS
illustrated by Sidney Levitt

Simon and Schuster Books for Young Readers • Published by Simon & Schuster Inc., New York

Father Rabbit was at work.
Mother Rabbit was cooking dinner.
The bunnies were looking out the window.
It was snowing hard.
Father Rabbit's train was late because of the snow.
He would not be home for dinner.

Honey Bunny and Sonny Bunny missed their father.
They worried about him as they watched the snow.
"May we have a tea party for Father when he comes
home?" Honey Bunny asked Mother Rabbit.
"Good idea," Mother Rabbit replied. "Hot tea will
be just right on a night like this."

Honey Bunny took out her china tea set.
The cups were white with tiny blue flowers on them.

Sonny Bunny, who was two years older, filled the kettle.
Mother Rabbit turned on the stove.

Honey Bunny spread a lace tablecloth on the table.
Sonny Bunny filled the sugar bowl and folded
the napkins.

Mother Rabbit said it looked just like a restaurant.

The bunnies pulled Father Rabbit's favorite chair over to the table.

They put his newspaper on the chair for him.
They made place cards for each guest.
Honey Bunny and Sonny Bunny kept getting new
ideas. Would they have enough time to do everything?

Sonny Bunny put Father's slippers next to his chair
while Honey Bunny went to get his warm robe.
Honey put her writing pad on the table. She
wanted to take Father's order like a waitress.

Sonny Bunny took Father Rabbit's favorite record album out and had it ready for him to play.

It was seven-fifteen.

The bunnies looked out the window to see if Father Rabbit was coming. All they saw was snow.

The bunnies were too excited to sit and wait.
"Let's bake a cake for Father," said Honey Bunny.

Soon they were as busy as could be. Honey Bunny
measured the flour. Sonny Bunny cracked the
eggs. Mother Rabbit greased the pan and turned on
the oven.

At eight-thirty the cake was done. But Father
still wasn't home.

Mother Rabbit said they could have some cake,
but the bunnies said no.

Not without Father.

The snow was getting deeper, and the bunnies
were getting tired.
They knew Mother Rabbit was worried because
they saw her looking out the window, too.

At nine o'clock Honey Bunny and Sonny Bunny
went to bed.

They said they would stay in bed but not fall asleep.
They wanted to be awake when Father Rabbit
came home.

They must have lost track of the time, because at nine-fifteen they were both sleeping.

At ten o'clock Father Rabbit came home.
He was tired. He was cold and wet.
He was hungry. He was sneezing and
blowing his nose. He was in a bad mood.
He told Mother Rabbit how bad his day had been.

Then he saw the table. He saw the tiny cups.
He saw the cake. He saw his favorite chair.
He saw his slippers, his robe, and his newspaper.
He smiled. He saw the waitress order pad.
He picked up his place card and read it...

Father Rabbit went into the bunnies' bedroom.
They were sound asleep.

He kissed each of them and pulled their covers up
so they would be nice and warm.

Then he tiptoed into the living room.
He put on his slippers and robe.
He sat in his favorite chair.

Mother Rabbit brought him a cup of tea in a big cup.
She cut him a piece of cake.

He picked up his newspaper and started to read.
His favorite record was playing softly.
He took a sip of the hot tea and forgot all about
his bad mood.

Honey Bunny and Sonny Bunny didn't know it then,
but they had made their father very happy that night.

The End

SIMON AND SCHUSTER BOOKS FOR YOUNG READERS
Simon & Schuster Building, Rockefeller Center, 1230 Avenue of the Americas, New York, New York 10020.
Text copyright © 1989 by Brian Mangas. Illustrations copyright © 1989 by Sidney Levitt.
All rights reserved including the right of reproduction in whole or in part in any form.
SIMON AND SCHUSTER BOOKS FOR YOUNG READERS is a trademark of Simon & Schuster Inc.
Designed by Mary Ahern. Manufactured in the United States of America.

10 9 8 7 6 5 4 3 2 1

Library of Congress Cataloging-in-Publication Data:
Mangas, Brian. A nice surprise for Father Rabbit/by Brian Mangas; illustrated by Sidney Levitt. 32 p.
SUMMARY: Two generous little bunnies give Father Rabbit a warm welcome home
on a cold winter night. (1. Rabbits—Fiction. 2. Parent and child—Fiction.)
I. Levitt, Sidney, ill. II. Title. PZ7.M312644Ni 1989
(E)—dc19   88-19764   CIP   AC   ISBN 0-671-67194-4